BOOKS
GIVE US
WINGS

2003-2004

St. Charles Public Library
Family Read-Aloud Book Club
Presented in honor of:

Lauren Nemer

Elvis the Camel

published by

Stacey International

128 Kensington Church Street

London W8 4BH

Tel: 020 7221 7166 Fax: 020 7792 9288

ISBN: 1 900988 39 9

CIP Data: A catalogue record for this book is available from the British Library

© Stacey International 2001

1 3 5 7 9 0 8 6 4 2

Design: Sam Crooks

Printing & Binding: Oriental Press, Dubai

Dedicated to all the animal lovers in the world, especially to Phyllis Hermann and her family: Dick, Otto, Annalis, and Karl.

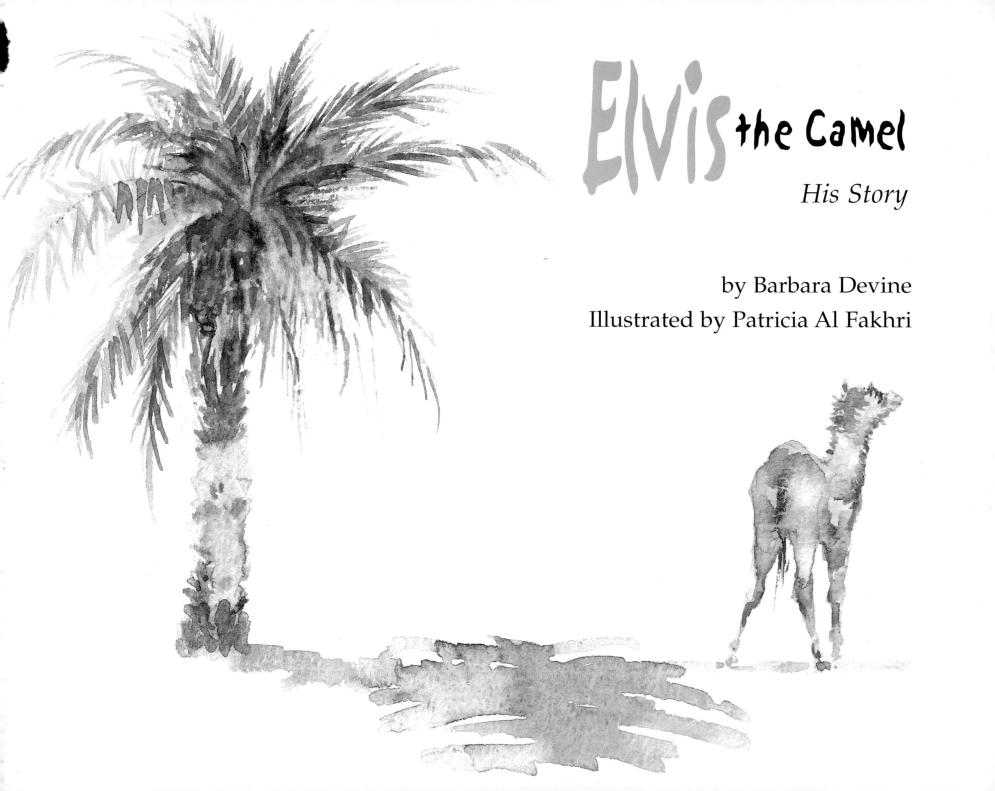

Elvis the Camel

His Story

by Barbara Devine

Illustrated by Patricia Al Fakhri

Camels once roamed freely over the sand. But change has
come. Roads, cars and trucks now mean danger for the camel.

When I was a baby, mother and I spent happy days and nights together. Her warm milk gave me strength.

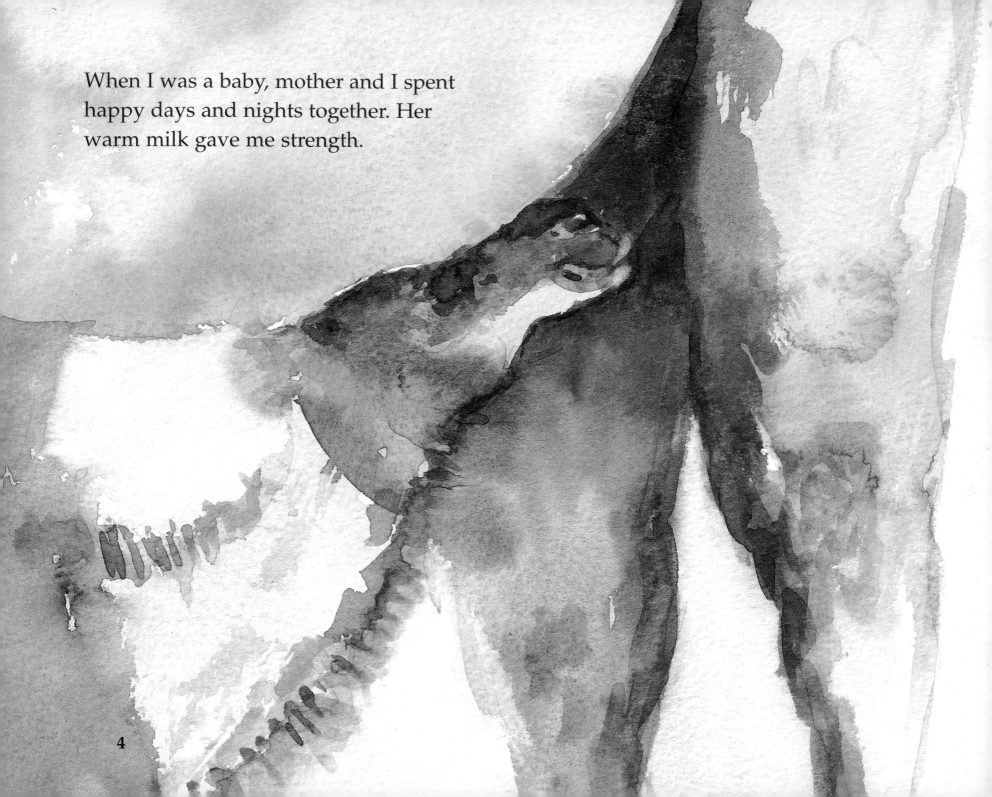

The bright sun, the blue sky and the
warm sand made me feel glad to be alive!
Mother blew air through her nostrils to
warm me in the cool evenings.

5

One night I was following mother. I felt the earth grow hard under my feet. The ground shook and there were bright, blinding lights... *yailah! yailah!*

6

The lights were coming at me! My legs froze with fear. I couldn't see mother. Was this a giant monster? Loud noise hurt my ears! *"Um! Um!"*

Then... only silence, darkness and pain...
I was alone. I hurt all over! I could not get up...

7

I lay alone on the cold sand all the long night. As the new day dawned, I heard sounds approaching. Was another monster coming? I trembled with fear.

Hands gently touched me. It was nothing but a hound dog and a lady. The dog sniffed me and whimpered. The lady made soft, comforting sounds.

Soon children came running with blankets and food. I was so hungry I ate some of the branches. The blankets warmed me. But where was mother? *"Um! Um!"* I wanted my mother!

Suddenly, I felt my mother's warm breath. Mother had found me at last! But, I could not stand up to drink her milk. The lady brought a bottle of milk which she put in my mouth. Most of it spilled, but it soothed my parched throat and eased my thirst.

Again, I tried to stand but couldn't. The lady needed to find a wise man, an expert with camels. Where could she look?

11

12

The camel race track, a place filled with camels and the people who tend to them. That was where they found him.

Yousef.

14

His hands were gentle. He showed the lady how to feed and burp me. He taught the children which shrub was my favourite.

Yousef and the others pulled up my back legs with a pole. The pain was terrible! I cried out!

16

Mother came charging down from
the sand dune where she had been
keeping watch over me.

17

Yousef slowly raised his hand to stop mother in her tracks. With a soft whisper, he calmed her. She seemed to understand he wanted to help.

After examining my injuries, Yousef said my hip was broken. He taught the family how to massage my hip and legs with a special ointment.

The daily routines began. Lifting with the pole, massaging, cleaning, and feeding. Yousef visited from time to time, giving helpful advice. Day by day I grew stronger.

Yet, I still could not walk. One day when a sandstorm suddenly swept the land, I wished I could be covered forever by the drifts.

Luckily, my new friends never gave up. They thought of using a hoist. It shook, rattled, and rolled me up until I was able to stand!

In this way I built up my legs, by standing for a short time each day.

20

Time went on until one day I could walk for a short distance all on my own!

Mother went to find the camel train.

21

While mother was gone I stayed with my new family. The children named me 'Elvis the Pelvis'. Their love helped me grow stronger.

22

One day I saw a camel train in the distance! Mother had come for me!

She had not forgotten me!
We were together again!

Friends are sad when they part.

Our herd travelled from place to place. Mother and I saw many sights. We saw villages where life is lived in the old way. We saw farms, race tracks and *souks* where goods and animals are sold in the open air. What a good life for camels!

And so time passed and I grew up. One day, a familiar sight came into view. Those smells! It was the home of my friends! I ran to find them.

Marhaba! *Marhaba*! My friends!

29

These days, the only reminder of my adventure is that my rock is a little rockier, and my roll is a little rollier, And, if you ever see my camel train, that's how you will know me, Elvis!

*Ma salama,
my friends,
Ma salama!*

Arabic vocabulary

Marhaba   Greetings

Um   Mother (the mother of Elvis would be
known as '*Um* Elvis'.)

Souk   Marketplace

Yallah!   Hurry!

Ma salama   farewell (go in safety)

The story of Elvis the Camel actually took place in the
United Arab Emirates. The family, with the help of
neighbours and wise Yousef, nursed Elvis back to
health after he was struck by a vehicle near their home.